Barbie™

MYSTERY FILES #6

The Clue in the Castle Wall

Want to read more of Barbie's Mystery Files? Don't miss the first book in the series, *The Haunted Mansion Mystery*.

Barbie™
MYSTERY FILES #6

The Clue in the Castle Wall

By Linda Williams Aber

SCHOLASTIC INC.

New York   Toronto   London   Auckland   Sydney
Mexico City   New Delhi   Hong Kong   Buenos Aires

For Richard, the king of Castle Mountford

ISBN 0-439-55709-7

Copyright © 2003 Mattel, Inc.
BARBIE and associated trademarks and trade dress are owned by, and used under license from, Mattel, Inc. All rights reserved.
Published by Scholastic Inc.
SCHOLASTIC and associated logos are trademarks and/or registered trademarks of Scholastic Inc.

Designed by Peter Koblish
Photography by Tom Wolfson, Sheryl Fetrick, Greg Roccia, Lawrence Cassel, Scott Meskill, Judy Tsuno, and Lisa Collins

12 11 10 9 8 7 6 5 4 3 2 1   3 4 5 6 7/0

Printed in the U.S.A.
First printing, December 2003

You can help Barbie solve this mystery! Flip to page 36 and use the reporter's notebook to jot down facts, clues, and suspects in the case. Add more notes as you and Barbie uncover clues. If you can figure out who the culprit is, you'll be on your way to becoming a star reporter, just like Barbie!

Chapter 1

• • • • • • • • • • • • • • • • • • • •

A ROYAL ASSIGNMENT

"Wow!" Barbie exclaimed. She stared out the car window. "Castle Mountford looks just like Cinderella's castle!"

"I can't believe we're in England," Christie said. "I have to get a picture of this!" She aimed her camera out her window and clicked.

"I can't believe we're here to meet royalty — and on our first assignment for a big magazine!" Barbie sighed.

The driver of their limousine cleared his throat. "Excuse me, miss," he said in a British accent. "Shall I drive on?"

Barbie laughed. "Oh, why yes, of course. Forgive us, Manning," she said. "We've never seen a real English castle before. It's all so exciting!"

"May I ask you a question, miss?" the driver asked. Barbie nodded. "Are you related to Princess Anna? A cousin, perhaps?"

"A relative of a princess? Me?" Barbie laughed. "Oh, gosh, no! I'm a newspaper reporter. This is Christie, my good friend and photographer. We are here to cover the story of Princess Anna's crowning ceremony."

"Oh, it's a story all right, miss," Manning replied. "In fact, it's a legend!"

"A legend?" Barbie asked, leaning forward in her seat to hear better.

"That it is, miss," Manning said. He steered the car down the long road to Castle Mountford. "Many, many years ago, a young man named Richard created some beautiful jewelry for the kings and queens in the land. When Richard delivered a necklace to the lady of this castle, he fell in love with her daughter, Princess Laura. Richard created the Star Sapphire Crown just for her."

"How romantic!" Barbie and Christie said together.

"Oh, yes," Manning continued. "But that's not the end of the story. Richard and Laura were married, and the crown stayed in their family for years and years. They had sons, and their sons had sons. At last a little girl was born. That girl is Princess Anna, who is to be presented with the crown on her twentieth birthday."

"What a beautiful story!" Barbie exclaimed.

"It's a real-life fairy tale," Manning replied.

Finally the car reached the end of the long drive. The doors to the castle opened. A tall woman with gray hair stepped outside. She came forward to greet Barbie and Christie.

As the woman came closer, her smile changed to a look of surprise. "Forgive me for my reaction," she said to Barbie. "It's just that . . . your appearance . . ."

Barbie blushed. Maybe she should have worn something fancier. "Oh, I'm sorry. . . ." she began.

Just then a young woman stepped outside. "Hello!" she called in a British accent.

Barbie and Christie gasped. Standing before them was a young woman who looked exactly like Barbie! They could be twins!

"Now you see what surprised me," the older woman said. "I was expecting you, of course. But I did not expect you to look so much like Anna! I'm Lady Dora Burke, and this is my niece, Anna Mountford."

"Princess Anna," Barbie said. "I'm Barbie

Roberts and this is my friend Christie. It's a pleasure to meet you."

Anna laughed. "The pleasure is mine," the princess replied. "But please, do call me Anna. I can tell we're going to be great friends."

"Like sisters," Lady Burke said, smiling.

"Oh, yes," Anna agreed, linking arms with Barbie and Christie. "*Just* like sisters."

Chapter 2

· ·

MRS. WHITCOMB

Anna was right. All three girls felt as if they'd been friends forever. All the talk over dinner was about the crowning ceremony.

"It will be a very important day for the Mountford family," Lady Burke explained. "The crown has been locked in a vault for a hundred years. Once a year, it is removed to be polished and cleaned. But midmorning tomorrow we shall all have a look at it. A jeweler is coming to stay at the castle to do the final fitting."

"What an exciting day it will be!" Anna exclaimed.

6

"Well, the sooner we all go to bed, the sooner tomorrow will come!" Lady Burke said.

Anna showed the girls to their rooms. They were in one of the round castle towers. Each room had round walls and windows. The beds were big and comfortable. They woke up ready to see the Star Sapphire Crown.

"Good morning!" Anna said at breakfast. "Did you sleep well?"

"Oh, yes," Barbie answered. "Very well. I hope there will be time to have a better look at your beautiful castle."

"But of course!" Anna replied. She and Lady Burke showed Barbie and Christie the ballroom, where kings and queens had danced. Then they took Barbie and Christie to the dining room, with its sparkling crystal. Next they saw the dozens of sitting rooms and big bedrooms on the upper floors.

"It's a lot of work for our housekeeper, Mrs. Whitcomb," Lady Burke said. She closed the door to the library and moved to the next room.

"I manage very well, my lady, thank you very much," said a voice behind them. The white-haired woman wearing an apron and cap raised her chin proudly. She looked surprised to see Barbie standing next to the princess, but made no comment.

"Of course you do," Lady Burke said. "Barbie, Christie, allow me to introduce Mrs. Whitcomb. She keeps the castle running like clockwork."

"So nice to meet you, Mrs. Whitcomb," Barbie said. "I hope we won't be adding too much extra work for you."

"That's not for you to worry, miss," Mrs.

Whitcomb replied coldly. She turned to Lady Burke. "The jeweler is waiting in the drawing room," she said. "Shall I open the vault now?"

"Yes, please, Mrs. Whitcomb," Lady Burke replied. "We'll join him. Please bring the crown to us in there."

"You'll show it to strangers, my lady?" Mrs. Whitcomb asked. She sounded displeased.

"These are reporters who have come all the way from America to interview us, Mrs. Whitcomb," Princess Anna said sweetly. "They are welcome to view the crown with us."

"Yes, Princess," the housekeeper said. "As you wish."

Lady Burke and Anna started down the hall. As they passed, Barbie heard Mrs. Whitcomb muttering. "Hmmph! It's not proper. The Mountford family shouldn't be showing off their jewels to commoners."

Barbie and Christie looked at each other, surprised. But Lady Burke and Anna hadn't heard the housekeeper. So the two friends followed their hosts to the drawing room. The jeweler was waiting there.

"Oh!" Princess Anna said, startled. "You're not the jeweler I expected!"

"Nor I," Lady Burke added.

This jeweler was not the old, white-haired man named Mr. Winston. Instead, a very handsome young man with dark hair and blue eyes was waiting for them.

"I'm William Winston," the young man said. "My father is ill. He has sent me in his place. Don't worry. I am qualified and trained by the best, my father."

Lady Burke looked worried. "The crown is

a treasure to the Mountford family. It must be handled with the greatest of care."

"You may be sure, Lady Burke," William Winston said. "I shall do my best. I would offer nothing less to a princess as lovely as Princess Anna."

Princess Anna blushed. But Barbie noticed something funny. For a jeweler who needed steady hands, William Winston seemed a little nervous.

Chapter 3

• • • • • • • • • • • • • • • • • • • •

THE STAR SAPPHIRE CROWN

Just then, Mrs. Whitcomb entered the drawing room. In her hands she held a blue velvet cushion. Resting on top was the legendary Star Sapphire Crown.

"How lovely!" Barbie exclaimed. "Perfectly lovely!"

"Amazing!" Christie added.

Mrs. Whitcomb placed the cushion down on a table close to the far wall. William Winston took out a fancy jeweler's glass. He examined the sapphires through it. "Exquisite!" he declared.

12

"May I photograph the crown?" Christie asked.

It was too much for Mrs. Whitcomb. "No!" she blurted out. "It's just not proper! Newspaper people! Strangers!"

"Of course you may," Lady Burke said. She turned to the housekeeper and said, "You may go now, Mrs. Whitcomb."

"Yes, my lady," Mrs. Whitcomb replied. She turned on her heel and marched out. She looked upset.

Christie took photos of the crown from every angle. Barbie wrote notes in her reporter's notebook.

"Here, here! What's all the fuss about?" A young man dressed in riding clothes entered the room. All attention turned to him.

"Cousin Guy!" Anna exclaimed. "You're just in time to see the crown."

13

"Oh, no," Guy said. "I'm not interested in that kind of thing. It's a great day for riding. Aren't you going to join me, Anna? And who are your lovely friends?"

Anna made the introductions. Guy bowed and kissed their hands. "Great to meet you, ladies," he said. "And you, too, William."

"But won't you stay?" Anna asked.

"Ha!" Guy laughed. "You should give up all this silly crown-worshipping and come riding with me. But if I can't convince you to join me, I'll be off." He disappeared down the hall.

"Pay no mind to cousin Guy," Anna said. "He's bound to show up again. He arrived out of nowhere, and now he seems to be planning on staying forever."

Christie went back to taking photos. Then she screamed. "It's gone!" she cried. "The crown is gone!"

Everyone stared at the spot where the crown had been. William Winston looked shocked. Lady Burke turned pale as she slumped to the velvet sofa.

"Auntie Dora!" Anna cried, rushing to her aunt's side.

Barbie's eyes were already scanning the room. A curtain on the wall by the table moved slightly. And was it her imagination or had the eyes of the portrait on the wall blinked?

Chapter 4

••••••••••••••••••••

BARBIE ON THE CASE

Barbie ran to the doorway to call Guy back. She saw a figure in the shadows in the hallway. "Guy?" she called out. "Is that you?"

"No it's not, Princess," the housekeeper answered, mistaking Barbie for Anna.

"Mrs. Whitcomb!" Anna cried, coming up behind Barbie. "Something terrible has happened. The crown! It's gone missing!"

"Oh, n-no, miss!" Mrs. Whitcomb stammered. "It should never have been out for strangers to see! It's a ghost that's taken it!"

"Don't be silly, Mrs. Whitcomb!" Lady

Burke said. She still looked a little shaky. "There are no ghosts at Castle Mountford! I'm sure it's all a mistake. Please come back into the drawing room."

"Oh, Auntie Dora!" Anna cried. "Whatever shall we do?"

"We must not tell anyone about this," Lady Burke said seriously. "It has to be kept a secret. We cannot call the police. A theft at the castle would be a huge disgrace to the Mountford name!"

"Is there anything I can do?" William asked.

"Barbie can help!" Christie announced. "She's solved lots of mysteries at home!"

All eyes turned to Barbie. But she was already working on the case. She was making quick notes in her reporter's notebook. *The Drawing Room: Present at the time of theft — Barbie, Christie, Princess Anna, Lady Burke, cousin Guy, William Winston.*

While the others looked for the crown under the furniture and behind the cushions, Barbie checked the curtain she'd seen moving. Only the paneled wall was behind it. There was no room for anyone to hide.

Then Barbie examined the portrait more closely. The eyes stared straight ahead. They did not move.

Barbie made a few more notes. Then she turned to Anna and Lady Burke. "Please try not to worry," she said. "Christie and I will do everything we can to help."

"Oh, how can we ever thank you?" Anna cried. She smiled through her tears.

Barbie smiled back at Anna. Then she made one more note in her notebook: *Things to Do: Solve the mystery of the missing Star Sapphire Crown.*

Chapter 5

• • • • • • • • • • • • • • • • • • • •

A LETTER
FROM PRINCESS LAURA

Barbie spent the rest of the day looking for clues. She was glad to climb into bed that night. But instead of resting peacefully, Barbie tossed and turned in her bed. She dreamed of a crown floating away and a castle filled with ghosts and strange noises. A loud bang woke her up. The light in the hall flickered, then went out.

"The power is out!" Barbie breathed.

Feeling her way along the wall to her tote bag, Barbie reached for a flashlight. "There!"

she said as the ring of light brightened the room.

She went to the window and pulled the banging shutter closed. She realized the strong wind must have blown down the power lines — and loosened the shutter. It was still pitch black, but Barbie shined the light all around. There was nothing there. But the beam of light found a small door on the wall in one corner. Barbie hoped it was a fuse box so she could turn the lights back on.

Barbie fumbled along the sides of the panel until it opened. Inside there was a single lever. "I wonder what this is?" she whispered. "It can't hurt to try it!"

Barbie pulled the lever. In an instant, the floor opened under her feet, and she dropped into a pit! Fortunately, she wasn't hurt. Barbie pointed her flashlight up. The walls surrounding her were about six feet high. A wooden ladder was attached to one side.

Barbie had read about tunnels like this. In the old days, when castles came under attack, people inside the castle could enter a secret tunnel from almost any room.

Barbie started to climb the ladder. Then she felt a cool breeze blowing on her neck. There was a tunnel opening behind her!

A yellowed envelope was sticking out from between two stones above the open tunnel. Inside was a letter that Barbie could tell was from long, long ago. The paper was crumbly, and the handwriting faded. *To the next princess,* the note said, *whoever she may be: The Star Sapphire Crown is my greatest treasure. If ever the crown is in danger, please keep it in my secret room, the last place to look.*

Barbie took a deep breath and entered the tunnel. She walked facing the stone wall, pressing her hands against it along the way. Suddenly, a section of the wall opened, and she was in a supply closet. There was a small panel on the wall. Sliding the panel aside, she found two eyeholes. Through those holes Barbie had a perfect view of the drawing room!

It wasn't my imagination! Barbie thought. *I really did see the eyes on the portrait move!*

To Barbie's surprise, someone entered the drawing room. He held a candle. "Cousin Guy!" she whispered. "What's he doing there at this time of night?"

Something startled Guy. He looked up and saw the jeweler in the doorway. He had decided to stay the night because of the bad weather. "Couldn't sleep," William said. "The wind is too loud."

"Same problem here," Guy said. "But off to bed I go again. See you in the morning."

Guy left. William picked a book off a shelf and left, too.

Barbie's flashlight was growing dimmer. She knew she had to get back to her room. She hurried through the tunnel. She reached the ladder to her room just as the light went out.

In complete darkness, Barbie climbed the ladder, pulled the lever to close the trapdoor, and got back into bed. Even the excitement of the night couldn't keep Barbie awake any longer. The letter from Princess Laura fell from her hand as Barbie drifted off to sleep.

Chapter 6

· · · · · · · · · · · · · · · · · ·

THE SECRET ROOM

By the time Barbie got up and ready for the day, Christie was already outside taking photos. Princess Anna and Lady Burke were outside by the car with Mrs. Whitcomb. There wouldn't be time to talk with them about her adventure. But she hurried outside to say good-bye.

"I feel sorry to leave you," Princess Anna said.

"But we must keep up appearances," Lady Burke added.

"Try not to worry," Barbie said. "You're leaving the castle in good hands, I promise."

24

"Of course she is, miss!" Mrs. Whitcomb snapped.

Anna and Lady Burke tried to hold their heads up high as the car drove away.

Mrs. Whitcomb went inside, and Barbie waited a few minutes before going in. As she headed toward the drawing room, a loud crash came from the room.

Barbie rushed to the doorway of the room. A vase lay in pieces on the floor. Guy was pulling the cushions off the couches. He dug his hands down into the backs of the chairs. "Where is it?" he muttered to himself. "Things don't disappear just like that!"

"Oh, trouble and bother, trouble and bother!" Mrs. Whitcomb wailed from the end of the hallway.

Guy looked up. "Drat!" he said. "Here comes Mrs. Whitcomb!"

The housekeeper appeared with the same broom and dustpan Barbie had seen in the closet the night before.

"What — oh!" Guy said, startled to see Barbie and the housekeeper. "Jolly good that you're both here. I believe I dropped something here and I was looking for it."

"The thing you've dropped, sir," Mrs. Whitcomb snapped angrily, "is a valuable vase that's been in the Mountford family for years!"

Quickly she swept up the blue, white, and gold pieces of the vase. "Done!" Mrs. Whitcomb said. "Now perhaps you'd better spend the rest of your day at the stables!"

Mrs. Whitcomb shooed Guy out the door. As soon as they were gone, Barbie walked over to the portrait on the wall. She wanted a second look at those eyes. But her foot caught on a sliver of the broken vase stick-

26

ing out from a crack in the floor. Barbie bent down to pick up the piece. As she picked it up, she discovered that the crack wasn't a crack at all. It was a perfect square, just the size of the trapdoor in her tower room! Just big enough for a person to fit through if he or she wanted to get out of the drawing room . . . or into it!

Barbie searched for the lever that would open the trapdoor. "Aha!" she cried. She pulled the lever, and the trapdoor opened. Barbie lowered herself into a tunnel.

A small light at the end of the tunnel lit the way. Barbie hurried toward the light. It led her to the very end of the tunnel and a secret door.

Barbie remembered Princess Laura's words in her letter: ". . . *my secret room, the last place to look.*" Was this that secret room?

The door was slightly open. Someone

was moving around in there! Very carefully, Barbie peeked in. It was a room fit for a princess. The walls were covered in pink-and-white satin. There was a love seat, a rocking chair, a dressing table and mirror, and a bed with a white lace canopy. The room was perfectly neat and looked as though it had not been disturbed in many years.

Barbie couldn't see who was in there. But she did see a sparkle of light coming from a table in the corner. It was the Star Sapphire Crown, safe in the secret room!

Barbie had to make a quick decision. Should she step inside the room and face the thief? Or should she go back through the tunnel and get help?

The decision was made for her when the secret door snapped shut in her face. Barbie heard footsteps going upstairs. Then there was silence. She pressed her hands on the wall. The secret door creaked open. Barbie stepped inside Princess Laura's secret room, the last place to look.

Chapter 7

• •

A CROWNING ACHIEVEMENT

Alone in the secret room, Barbie took a moment just to look around. Everything was beautiful. Everything was peaceful. It was indeed a room where a princess would feel safe.

Barbie's plan was to take the crown and slip out again through the tunnel. But before she could, she heard footsteps on the stairs again. This time, the thief was coming back to the secret room!

Thinking fast, Barbie grabbed the crown and placed it in plain view on the floor of a large closet. She had just enough time to hide herself behind the open door of the closet. If her plan worked, she would save the crown and catch the thief!

Barbie waited. Something dropped and rolled near Barbie's hiding place. She looked down and saw a crown-shaped cuff link. Where had she seen one like that before?

Cousin Guy! she realized. *He was wearing those cuff links the day the crown was stolen!*

So it was Guy after all, she thought. *That's why he showed up at the castle. And that's why he pretended he didn't care about the crown. He was planning to steal it all along!*

Just as Barbie thought she had the whole thing figured out, the person in the room sneezed. "Oh, good gracious, there can't be dust in this room!" the voice said.

It was Mrs. Whitcomb! She came closer

31

to the open door of the closet and saw the crown. "Now how in the world did you get in there?" she said. "I put you on the desk myself!"

Barbie could wait no longer. She stepped out and stood in the shadow of the closet door.

"Princess Anna!" Mrs. Whitcomb declared when she saw Barbie. "I thought you were out for the day, miss."

Mrs. Whitcomb thought she was Princess Anna! Barbie decided to play along for a while. "Oh, no. I've come back, Mrs. Whitcomb," she said in her best British accent. "I've come for my crown, the one you stole!"

"But I did it for you, miss!" the house-keeper cried. "I did it for the Mountford family! It's not proper to display our treasures for photographers and reporters!"

Barbie dropped her fake accent and her disguise. "Reporter?" Barbie asked. "Do you mean me?"

Mrs. Whitcomb turned pale. She'd been caught! The housekeeper turned and rushed up the stairs. Barbie heard a door snap closed.

Barbie took the crown and followed Mrs. Whitcomb up the stairs. She came to a door like many others she had seen. She knew exactly where to press to make the door open. And when it did, Barbie found herself standing inside the supply closet!

Barbie heard voices on the other side of the wall. She opened the panel with the eyeholes and peeked through the portrait's eyes into the drawing room. There was Mrs. Whitcomb surrounded by Princess Anna, Lady Burke, Guy, William, and Christie. "And then I saw her with the crown pretending

33

to be Princess Anna!" the housekeeper was saying. "She's the one! It's the reporter!"

"I think not!" Barbie said through the eyeholes of the portrait.

All eyes turned to the portrait. "Barbie?" Christie said, staring up at the eyes of the picture.

Barbie winked at her friend. "I'll be there in the wink of an eye!" she said.

Barbie walked out the closet door and into the drawing room. She carried the crown to its rightful owner, Princess Anna. She also returned the crown cuff link to Guy.

"You found what I was searching for!" he said.

"I think Mrs. Whitcomb found it, actually," Barbie said. "Perhaps she was starting a crown collection!"

Barbie went on to explain about the letter

she'd found. "It was the clue in the castle wall that helped me find the secret room and the crown," she said. "Mrs. Whitcomb confessed everything when she thought she was speaking to Anna."

"I shall deal with Mrs. Whitcomb properly," Lady Burke said. "Perhaps she did have the best intentions."

"Oh, yes, my lady," Mrs. Whitcomb cried.

Princess Anna gave Barbie a big hug. "Thank you, Barbie," she said sincerely. "You saved the day for the Mountford family!"

"Hold that pose, please!" Christie said. "It's not every day I get to photograph two princesses at once!"

Barbie and Princess Anna looked at each other and smiled.

Reporter's Notebook

Can YOU solve the mystery of *The Clue in the Castle Wall*? Read the notes in Barbie's reporter's notebook. Collect more notes of your own. Then, YOU solve it!

Story Assignment: Go to Castle Mountford in England. Meet Princess Anna. Learn the history of the Star Sapphire Crown. Report on the crowning of the princess.

• •

Background Info:
• Years ago, a jeweler named Richard fell in love with Princess Laura. He made her the Star Sapphire Crown and asked for her hand in marriage. The crown has been in the Mountford family for years. Now the crown will be given to the new princess, Anna.
• Just days before the crowning, the Star Sapphire Crown disappears!

```
Mystery:
```

Who: Who stole the crown?

What: What is cousin Guy looking for in the drawing room? What is the "last place to look"?

Where: Where does the tunnel go?

Why: Why are cousin Guy and William Winston both up late in the drawing room?

```
Facts and Clues:
```

• Cousin Guy arrived suddenly and seems to plan on staying.

• Cousin Guy is searching for something in the drawing room.

• The regular jeweler has sent his son, William, in his place.

• The eyes of the portrait on the wall seem to move.

• Mrs. Whitcomb is unfriendly to guests.

• There is a secret letter.

• Tunnels under the castle lead to every room.

Suspects:
• Cousin Guy
• Mrs. Whitcomb
• William Winston

Additional Notes:

Clue #1 _____

_____

_____

Clue #2 _____

_____

_____

Clue #3 _____

_____

_____

Clue #4 _____

_____

_____

Clue #5 _____

_____

_____

Clue #6 _____

_____

_____

Now YOU Solve It!

CONGRATULATIONS from BARBIE! You are an Official Star Reporter and Mystery Solver! Sharpen your mystery-solving wits and get ready to help Barbie solve her next big case.